Hope and Jazzy

Book #1

Boxcar to Nowhere

Hope and Jazzy

Boxcar to Nowhere

Arcus Verba Publishing
P.O Box 210
De Forest, Wisconsin
53532
www.arcusverba.com

Cover design by Alexander Francis
Graphic images by Alexander Francis

ISBN: 978-1-942420-31-6 print edition
ISBN: 978-1-942420-32-3 e-book

Novels by Alexander Francis

Revenge of Jesus

Since Antonius

Are We A Band Yet

Mick Grundy…Spy Hunt

Mick Grundy…The Russian Connection

Mick Grundy…Elapid

Geminknot

Beware The Exit

The Green Scarf

Memory Gap

The Copy Candidate

Spook, my best friend

Please visit afnovels.com for more information

FORWARD

Hope and Jazzy book #1 is the first of a series which will pair fifteen year old, Hope Baros, daughter of a working policeman, and a formidable German Shepherd, a retired police dog with years of experience. Jazzy lives with Hope and her Dad and has become the constant companion of Hope. This book, and future ones in this series, are about their relationship and their mutual adventures.

This series has been created for the enjoyment and vicarious adventure of young teenagers who share a love of dogs and muse about exploring life with one at their sides for both companionship and possible protection.

I have taken the liberty to make the place and era of this book non-specific because trust between master and dog is forever timeless. The often quoted expression 'man's best friend' is indeed true, and we will see that expression come to life many times in this book and in the ones to follow.

Alexander Francis

TABLE OF CONTENTS

Chapter One

Breakfast in a Hurry

Hope could feel her father's warm breath against her cheek and realized that he was whispering and gently shaking her shoulder.

"Wake up, my sweet Hope," he said. "Gotta get up early today because I've got to go in pretty soon." Hope rubbed her eyes with her fists and slowly sat up, looking around.

"Hi, Pop," she mumbled. While speaking, she looked down at the floor beside her bed, expecting the big dog to be looking back. He wasn't there. "Where is Jazzy?"

"Oh, I let him out when I came up. He'll be back in the kitchen when you come down. I put breakfast on the table for you, so there's only getting your drink for you to do. I'll call you later and check in."

"Wait, Pop," she said, realizing what he just said. "You mean you are going to work this early?"

"Sure I am. Where else would I go and leave you alone?" Pop laughed and kissed her cheek briefly before standing erect. Hope noticed that his policeman hat was already on his head, and his badge over his left shoulder was shining in the morning sun.

"Can you tell me why?" Hope asked.

"Oh, some guy broke out of jail, and they think they have him cornered somewhere near the rail yards. They need a lot of us to cover that area so he can't get away." Hope nodded and slid off the bed, thinking about what she should wear.

“Well, goodbye, my girl,” Pop said, turning to leave her bedroom. “Love ya.” Pop glanced over his shoulder at her and winked, then ambled off.

“Love you, too!” Hope yelled as he disappeared. She heard his footsteps on the stairs and then the outside door closed behind him.

Hope sat back down on the bed and tried to think about today. Her plans had been changed with Pop gone. She stood again and started dressing while thinking about Jazzy. Where was he…did he get back inside? Out of the corner of her eye she caught some movement near the door and looked that way. Jazzy was looking directly at her, a smile on his face, as he made his way to her side. After touching her leg with his muzzle, he sat down and looked silently at her face, intense love written all over him.

Hope reached down and stroked his big head and felt him push up against her hand as if to stroke back. At least big old Jazzy was there, always and forever.

He was hers, completely, and he was the one who decided that it should be so.

"I assume that you haven't been fed yet," Hope said aloud. "And you want to have your breakfast when I have mine. Isn't that so?" Jazzy responded with a small grunt, his mouth open to allow that big tongue to hang out. Hope finished dressing while Jazzy sat there, never looking at anything but her.

Jazzy wasn't an overly affectionate dog. He would allow petting, constantly, if that is what Hope wanted. But he was happy just being around her, watching her work or study but giving her enough space to not feel burdened or overwhelmed by him. When he came into her life permanently two years ago, Hope didn't fully understand how to treat him. Pop had, on a couple of occasions, alluded to the years Jazzy had spent on the police force, but it was Pop's friends in the force who took her aside to fully inform her of this dog's history of taking down bad guys. It seemed that Jazzy was something of a legend. Once, this single dog disabled three criminals attempting to flee from police. Two of them were hospitalized afterwards. Hope understood that they were warning her to be careful with him, and they had concerns that this particular dog should not be allowed to be unsupervised around a youngster like her.

At first, Hope was a bit fearful of Jazzy but that soon changed. It became obvious that she had been adopted by Jazzy, not the other way around. She was his, and he always made sure that nothing happened to her. She was never out of his watchful eye or out of range of his big erect ears. Jazzy was born in Germany, bred for his existence as a *Schutzhund*, the German equivalent of an American military canine. Most German Shepherds are a bit intimidating to people not used to them, but Jazzy was especially so with his large head, his penetrating dark eyes and his mottled black coat. All Jazzy had to do was to intently stare at someone for them to want to back away quietly, but none of Hope's friends had ever had the 'treatment'. Jazzy ignored them, tolerated their touching and patting him, and, in general, made himself scarce. He was always there though, the big eyes on the love of his life, his ears following her every utterance.

It didn't take long for Hope to realize his intelligence and his comprehension of her speech or her wants. He seemed to always know what she intended, even, on occasion, before she thought of it herself. Seeing his face when she left for school made her understand the agony Jazzy was experiencing watching her leave the house without him beside her. She would often bend down and stroke his neck, putting her cheek against his and telling him she loved him. Jazzy didn't need to speak to tell her he felt the same way. It was in his eyes.

They started breakfast across the room from one another, each frequently glancing at the other, assuring themselves that they were both safe and together. Hope looked longingly out the window and sighed, because the outing she planned with her father was now just evaporated plans, given up because of a call to duty. Hope sighed again, this time with more conviction, and let her shoulders sag a bit. She felt Jazzy's nose before she realized that he had come to her and was pushing his head into her lap. He held his position and looked up at her as if asking what he could do to make her happy.

"Oh, Jazzy, what would I do without you?" Hope said as she stroked his head, pushing his ears backward with her hand. A bell rang and Jazzy jerked his head around to confront whomever or whatever made the sound.

"It's just the front doorbell, Jazzy," Hope explained and then got up and headed that way, Jazzy right by her side.

Hope opened the door as Jazzy's nose and head pushed into the opening. A police officer was standing there smiling broadly.

"Hi," he offered, while glancing nervously at Jazzy who was now between Hope and this interloper, looking silently at his face. "You are Hope, I am informed," he asked, "and this is the famous Jazzy." It was more of a fact than a question. Dave looked her over while waiting for her answer. She was in her mid-teens, probably about the tenth grade or so…and lovely beyond words. He had no idea that old Gabe Baros had raised such a beauty, and all by himself. Hope was wearing a white, fashionable, summer button up sweater, and her blonde hair was pulled back into a pony tail. She fixed him with her clear blue eyes before responding.

Hope nodded that it was true but was reluctant to say more. She started thinking ahead, and the first thing that popped into her mind was that something had happened to her father.

"I should explain," the policeman said. "Sergeant Baros, your dad, asked me to come over here and bring Jazzy back to the search area. He said that Jazzy would help us to find the fugitives. I should tell you that I am a certified police dog handler, and I will be responsible for Jazzy. And, you can call me Dave. Everybody else does." He smiled and from somewhere produced a dog collar and leash that he held in view.

"I don't think that will work, Dave," Hope informed him. "Jazzy is retired and now is my dog."

"Yes, I was told that. But your dad said that it would only be for this morning and then we'll return him to you with our thanks. I've heard that your dog is the best tracker around and…," he trailed off as he looked at Jazzy. Something had changed, and he knew enough about dogs to understand when he was being threatened.

Hope glanced down and saw what was happening. She put her hand on Jazzy's nose and patted it gently. "You can tell that this dog is not going anywhere without me, can't you?"

“I can for sure see that,” he answered. “But your dad said…,” he stammered, not knowing how to handle this situation. He could see that it would be dangerous to attempt to collar this particular dog without his consent.

“We’ll both go with you. Will that be OK?” Hope suggested, then smiled, knowing this was the only way they were going to get Jazzy to work for them. At last she would get a firsthand look at police work. This was going to be an exciting day.

Chapter Two

Working the Line

Hope and Jazzy sat in the back seat of the cruiser driven by Dave, who was very talkative. He seemed nervous about what would be said regarding him escorting a minor to a manhunt.

"Well, Miss Hope, we'll find your Dad first and let him decide how to handle this."

"I prefer just 'Hope', if you don't mind," she retorted. She could see Dave nod his head, and they continued across town without another word from either of them. Hope had plenty of time to study this young policeman while he drove. She figured that Dave was fresh out of training, because he looked a bit too young to take him seriously…as a cop, that is. Jazzy sat beside her, content to just observe the town as it slid by the windows. He was certainly at home in the back of a squad car.

As they turned into the railroad yards, Hope could see a dozen police cars parked at odd angles and uniformed officers as well as plain clothed detectives. Some were walking up and down by the lines of parked freight cars stretching into the distance. Others were standing in small groups, and several of those held long guns pointing at the ground. Nearly all of them looked up and watched as the three exited the patrol car. Hope could hear murmuring as they observed her fasten the leash on Jazzy and head their way.

"Hey, Miss," one called out while moving toward her. "I recognize Jazzy, but can I ask who you are?" He smiled at her and stopped short, waiting for a reply. Dave caught up to her and laughed, expecting as much.

“Hi, Officer Matthews,” Dave said. “Sorry, but it was both of them or none. Not much choice. Do you know where Sergeant Baros is at the moment?” Matthews pointed and then turned away. Dave signaled Hope to follow and headed toward the railcars. “Sure you don’t want to let Jazzy come with me?” he asked with a sideways glance.

“You mean you would dare to try to take Jazzy from me?” she retorted, humor in her voice. Jazzy seemed interested and looked between them but stayed close alongside Hope’s leg. Dave didn’t respond, already knowing his answer was a loud ‘no’. After a short walk, they could see the other side of a big rusted boxcar. When other policemen came into view, they noticed Sergeant Baros was already headed toward them.

“Hope, you are not allowed to be here. We’ll take Jazzy, but I expect you to wait in the car until I get someone to drive you home.” Hope suddenly welled up with tears but otherwise tried not to show her disappointment.

Pop reached for the leash and looked down at Jazzy. It was a sight he had never seen before, at least on his side of the leash. Jazzy was very aware of what was happening but wanted no part of it. His ears were flat, and his teeth were showing. Pop dropped the leash and stepped back. "That's a surprise!" he remarked, then scratched the back of his head.

"Jazzy, *Fuss*," Sergeant Baros said loudly and authoritatively, expecting Jazzy to come to heel and await further commands. Jazzy was watching and listening attentively but didn't change his position beside Hope.

Dave spoke up, "Same thing with me. That's a dog who understands us plain enough but isn't about to leave his master."

“I have an idea, Pop,” Hope said a bit hesitantly. “Let me and Jazzy help search. You know with him around, I’ll be safe enough.”

“Yeah, yeah,” Pop said. He looked around thinking it out. They needed Jazzy, that was certain. But letting a 15 year old girl search for one, or possibly two, desperate men…no, that was not in the regulations, nor did it meet even common sense. “Say, Hope, what about you ordering Jazzy to come with me. I think that once out of your sight, he will start working like the police dog he is and used to be. How about giving it a try?”

Hope squatted beside Jazzy, her slender arm draped over his neck, and spoke into his ear, “Jazzy, you need to go with Pop. Do what he tells you, please.” She stood up and offered the leash to her dad. Then the growling started, low at first, becoming louder and more fierce. Jazzy lowered his head and fixed both policemen in a glaring stare. “Stop that, Jazzy!” Hope said loudly. The growling stopped abruptly but not the ‘look’. Hope stroked his head and pointed to her dad. “Now go to Pop and quit complaining.” Jazzy shot her a quick look but remained motionless. He was not going and that was final.

“Hey, what about that dog? Can we start working now or not?” was heard in the distance, and they all looked in the direction of the voice. Several men were motioning with their hands, meaning to move in their direction.

Pop looked angry and embarrassed at the same time. He turned in a complete circle out of frustration, trying to figure out some way to separate his daughter and her devoted guardian. This dog was smart, nearly human smart. He knew exactly what was happening and what was expected, no question about it. Time, though, was not on their side. They had to find the fugitives and the sooner the better.

Dave spoke up. “Sergeant, let me go with her, and I’ll be responsible for both of them.” He smiled at Hope and waited for a response.

“There isn’t much choice, is there?” Pop grumbled. “Go ahead then and take the lead, but be sharp, be ready. This could get serious.” Pop pointed toward the policemen standing by the rear of the first boxcar.

The three of them started off with Jazzy leading the way. Jazzy knew exactly what was expected of him, and with Hope close by, he was ready for anything. The group ahead spread apart and watched them arrive. Heads were shaking, and faces were glum, but they needed this dog, this particular dog, to go ahead of them and find the fugitives with his ears and nose. Something only a trained and gifted dog could do.

Chapter Three

FUGITIVE SEARCH

The small group closed around Captain Martinez who quickly gave orders, pointing to the men one at a time and directing them according to his strategy. Two were paired and assigned to start forward on one side of the long line of boxcars and two were chosen for the other side. He looked at the remaining three who were perhaps the most important: Dave, Hope and, of course, Jazzy. The three studied him in turn, silently awaiting his orders.

"I don't like this a bit. A young girl and a retired canine unit going out with a fledgling dog handler. What has happened to our police force…?" he complained aloud. "So…you three are to start searching for scent trails on the left side. If you find a hot trail, signal by hand gestures, and we will move closer to you. Hope…that *is* your name?" he asked and received a nod from her. “You have to take the leash off of Jazzy, and he will know what to do. Just follow him and stay alert. If there is any gunfire, then you are to drop to the ground at once and get as low as possible. You understand?” he asked sternly. Hope nodded that she understood, but she could feel her mouth start to dry out. She bent down and unclipped Jazzy who seemed to expect it and didn’t change his position.

“Officer Wentworth,” he said, addressing Dave. “There is a plastic bag over there which contains clothing of the fugitive. Have your dog study it and then start your search.”

It only took a few seconds for Jazzy to study the clothing with his nose, then, without any command, he started moving along the rail bed, his nose to the ground. Occasionally, Jazzy would stop, raise his head, sniff the air and look around, then, just as abruptly, drop his nose close to the ground and continue moving steadily forward.

“He really knows what he’s doing,” Dave observed to Hope. “I heard about this one, how relentless he is. They say he never fails.” Dave spoke in a low voice, his head close to Hope’s ear. She glanced at him but didn’t speak because she had heard those stories many times and utterly believed them. She and Dave walked together and followed Jazzy, who was ahead by twenty feet or so. Hope noticed that Dave also had a gun in his holster, and the two officers nearby carried long guns.

Once Jazzy got a positive scent, things abruptly started happening. Jazzy moved much quicker, his head up as he was able to pick up the scent from the air. Their fugitive was probably close by, and the thought of it brought an extra surge of excitement and fear. Hope had no idea of what could happen next.

“The man we are searching for is called Jerome Tate. He concealed himself in a garbage truck to get out of the prison last night and was spotted near here early this morning," Dave said, using a low voice. "We are not sure if he has a weapon, and we are not sure if someone is with him. If he had help, he may have a gun, so when things start to happen, I want you to back away as far as you can."

"Do you think he would shoot at us, or Jazzy?" Hope asked quietly and studied Dave's face. He shrugged. Clearly he didn't know either. Hope had never been in a risky situation before, and her anxiety grew more intense by the moment. She could see Jazzy occasionally look back at her, assuring himself that she was close by and in no danger.

Suddenly, Jazzy stopped, his full attention directed at a nearby boxcar. He was staring at the door intently, his ears focused on it as well. Hope could plainly see that the boxcar door was closed.

"Stay here, Hope," Dave ordered and started to cautiously move forward, silently drawing his pistol as he approached the door. The other policemen pointed their rifles at the door. One of them called out loudly using his hand as a megaphone: "Tate…we have you covered. Come out now and keep your hands up." The team expectantly waited for a response, but there was none. The boxcar remained silently immobile, the door closed as if it had always been parked harmlessly there. Jazzy had not moved from his spot and was focused on the door, his muscles tensed for a sudden appearance of the fugitive named Tate. It was obvious that something was about to happen, and Hope started to back away and lowered herself close to the ground.

One of the officers suddenly jerked open the big sliding door and stepped aside, just in time to miss being hit by two loud gunshots coming from inside the boxcar. There was another noise coming from the boxcar just before Jazzy jumped into the open door and disappeared inside. From her low position, Hope could see between the big steel wheels to the other side of the tracks. A pair of human legs appeared on the opposite side and began moving away. Nearly at the same time she saw Jazzy hit the ground and move rapidly in the same direction. Almost instantly, there were growls mixed with screams and feet and legs of uniformed officers moving in that direction, then quiet. The chase was over.

Chapter Four

A Moving Prison

Jazzy returned to Hope's side from under the boxcar. He had a worried look, an embarrassed look, as he came up to her, positioning himself beside her right leg, occasionally glancing up to her face as if to apologize for leaving her alone. Hope stroked his head, then bent down to embrace his neck. "You were magnificent, Jazzy. I'm so proud...." As she caressed him, the three policemen disappeared around the end boxcar, joining the others as they all gathered to get a look at the captured fugitive. Hope glanced around, realizing that she and Jazzy were alone, all the voices and laughs were coming from the other side. Up the line, boxcars seemed to stretch into the distance and around the curve, obscuring the endpoint, if there even was one. Alongside the tracks, trees and brush grew closer to the cars, making it seem even more ominous and mysterious.

Hope took a deep breath, the excitement of it all dissipating slowly. Her adventure was over for now, and she was going to be glad to shortly return home. She wondered if her dad would be returning with her or was the handsome young Dave going to be the one. She felt a tug and noticed that Jazzy was standing erect and looking down the long line of boxcars. He looked back at her for a moment, then gently started pulling her down the track in the opposite direction of the gathered police force. She felt like protesting because she really didn't want to go down the lonely track, away from protection. But Jazzy seemed to be purposely heading in that direction, and she unwillingly followed along, attached by the leash in her hand.

Hope could see that Jazzy was following his nose but keeping his head high and his ears trained ahead, alert to any sounds or scents. She recalled him sniffing the garments supplied before the search started. The fugitive had been caught already…or…

maybe not. She, for sure, didn’t want to track down a hostile bad man all by herself. Then she thought back on the events just before the big sliding door was pulled open. Jazzy might have been alerted to the presence of a man inside, not his scent. Were there two of them, after all? Could she now be pursuing the other one, even the escaped one? Alarms sounded in her head…she and Jazzy were now too far from the policemen to call out…and any cries for help might just alert the man Jazzy is pursuing. What to do?

Captain Martinez could see their captive locked in the back seat of a nearby cruiser. His head was down, and Martinez guessed that he was handcuffed with hands behind him. Martinez had seen the blood on his legs and arms from the dog attack earlier but only from a distance. “Drive our prisoner to the Emergency Room for treatment and then take him to the police station. Make sure he doesn’t escape.” He nodded at four men, easily enough to be safe. He looked around one last time. The entire train schedule had been interrupted because of this pursuit. Time to get things moving again, he thought. "Sergeant Baros," Martinez yelled, "Call the local Control Office and tell them they can resume activity."

Baros looked around at the assembly of men, studying their faces. They were thinking what he was…there may be another perp nearby, the one who had supplied the weapon and transportation. He had to be brought in as well. When he looked back toward the Captain to raise this issue, Baros could see him getting into a patrol car. As far as the Captain was concerned, the chase was over. Baros shrugged. He would make the call as requested.

Approaching the boxcar three down from the one which had contained the fugitive, Jazzy suddenly slowed. Hope could see his head looking not only under the cars but up at the top of them. He seemed to have crouched a bit, though he was still moving forward, being careful not to cause any sound. Hope picked her way over the loose gravel, also trying to be as silent as possible. She realized that, with her white sweater and blonde hair, she was highly visible, a target if there ever was one. She felt like running away, leaving Jazzy to handle this alone. But something inside told her that while running, she would be totally alone. Both choices were bad. She decided to stay with Jazzy who obviously was in control and used to this. Her pet knew more about hunting criminals then she ever would.

This time, the big sliding door was partially open, and Jazzy came to a stop right in front of it. His full attention focused on whatever was inside waiting for them. Hope could feel her hands start to sweat. She wished that she never wanted this adventure or went with Dave, so insolently, so confidently. The real world is indeed a frightening place.

Jazzy turned to look at her for a long moment, then quickly returned to watching the dark interior of the boxcar. After a couple of repeats, Hope got the message. Jazzy wanted his leash removed. He was going inside. Quickly reasoning it out, Hope agreed that Jazzy could act quicker without restraint of any kind. She unsnapped the leash and moved aside. Almost instantly, Jazzy made the big jump and was inside the boxcar. Hope covered her ears expecting gunfire again. She backed away, not knowing anything else she could do. There were faint sounds of Jazzy walking back and forth inside the car. The man they sought would have been attacked by now if he was inside. Trembling, she came back to the car and peeked inside, letting her eyes adjust to the dark interior. Jazzy was pacing, his nose to the deck, and he kept returning to one spot. That was at the foot of a steel ladder which led to the roof opening. The man Jazzy sought must have gone up the ladder.

"Jazzy, here!" she called softly, wanting him to come to her and give up the chase. Once more, Jazzy circled the interior coming to rest beneath the ladder, expectantly looking up at the closed hatch. He barked loudly in frustration, ignoring Hope's command. Reluctantly, Hope found a short ladder meant to assist climbing into the car. She had to go fetch Jazzy and put on his leash, otherwise he showed no willingness to give up the chase. Once in the car, she looked around, taking in all the corners…just in case. It was empty except for small piles of straw in the corners. No hiding bad men were in there, and she started to relax. She clipped the leash to Jazzy's collar and tugged him toward the door. "Come, Jazzy," she commanded.

After a pause, Jazzy turned to go with her. There in the partially opened sliding door was a man's head and shoulders. He was grinning at them. Jazzy leaped at the door, ripping the leash from Hope's hand just as the door slammed shut, forcing Jazzy to bank off the closed door. He spun around, all teeth showing while growling a deep threatening rumble. To no avail. The door was closed, and they were inside, the man outside. When she reached the door, Hope tried in vain to open it, but it wouldn't budge…the door was locked from the outside. Before she could think it out, there was a jerk and clanking from the train. It was underway, and they were trapped inside, on their way to someplace distant. It had to be Jerome Tate who was trying to keep Jazzy from tracking him. He was definitely on the train as they all rattled into the unknown.

Chapter Five

Where is Hope?

Sergeant Baros watched as the two patrol cars drove in and parked side by side. Through one car window he could see white bandages on the prisoner in the back seat. Brad Stiller was the first to emerge, and he greeted Baros with a wave. “Sorry we took so long but they were busy in the ER. Here he is, finally. Good luck with him. We couldn’t get a word out of him other than complaints.”

The captive was assisted out of the back seat, and Sergeant Baros got his first complete look. There was a large bandage covering his lower right arm, one circling his lower leg, and an extensive one covering his neck. Sergeant Baros raised his eyebrows and stroked his chin. A few more seconds and Jazzy would have killed this one. He obviously was trying to do just that.

With two officers helping, the prisoner was led into the police station and down to the nearest interview room. As soon as the man was seated, he glared at the officers and shook his head. "I'm telling you nothing until I get a lawyer. Don't bother to ask." One of the men handed Sergeant Baros an envelope marked 'evidence'. Baros opened it and poured the contents on the desk in front of the prisoner. One of the items was a very scuffed wallet.

Baros pulled out the identification cards, inspected them quietly, then a worried look came over his face. "Says here that you are Tommy Thomson…two cards have that name. Where did you get this wallet?" The captive had no comment and continued to glare at Baros, defiantly not willing to answer any questions. Baros thought about this new identity emerging just at this moment. This suspect was presumed to be Tate, the escaped convict, but this man's clothing was well worn, not new, and so was the wallet.

Baros pulled one of the officers aside. “Better get a photo of Tate and bring it in here…something’s wrong.” He tossed the wallet back into the envelope and sat down. “One question, and you better answer it…is your name Jerome Tate?” Again the defiant glare but no response. Baros crooked his finger at the other officers, “Book this one as unidentified and get his prints right away.” They understood and rapidly assisted the suspect to his feet and led him away.

Sergeant Baros was left alone in the room with nothing but the remaining contents of the man’s pockets scattered on the table. He had become convinced that this was not the fugitive Tate but the one helping him to escape, the one who had provided the transportation, clothing and possibly a weapon or two. If that was true, then the fugitive Tate was still on the run and possibly had evaded their local police force. Their efforts had been concentrated in the local railway yard where it is possible Tate intended to hitch a ride on a departing train. Baros himself had watched one train slowly pulling away after permission had been given. He banged his fist on the table in exasperation. The arrest had been flubbed, the man named Tate had escaped to parts unknown.

“He’s not Tate,” the officer said as he placed the photo on the desk, and one glance certified that that statement was, unfortunately, true. Jerome Tate was on the move, thanks to a hasty conclusion.

Baros looked up, nodding his head in agreement. “Yes, we made a premature assumption, but at least we caught his assistant and perhaps we can get useful information from him that might determine where Tate is headed.” Baros got up and recalled that he had not had a cup of coffee in hours, and he headed to the break room. Three officers were already doing the same thing, enjoying their coffee, when Baros came in. The abrupt way they stood up and watched him indicated that they had been discussing the morning’s activities among themselves.

“So, you guys have something to say to me?” Baros asked over his shoulder while pouring a cup. He turned around and inspected them one by one, waiting on a reply.

“Sarge, we were all impressed by your daughter this morning, no doubt about it. She showed a lot of courage just being there. And thanks to her dog, Jazzy, we caught the fugitive quicker than we thought. Plus, are you aware of just how beautiful she has become?” one of them asked, suppressing a small laugh as he spoke.

“Hope is becoming a woman under my very eyes. Every day she changes, and it won’t be much longer and she will be gone from me. I do indeed notice how she looks, and it always hits me how much like her mother she has become,” Baros admitted. “But enough of that, we just discovered that the man we captured is not the escapee from prison. We have not caught Tate, at least not yet.”

There was surprise and dismay on all three of their faces. They looked back at Sergeant Baros, not knowing what to say. “What do we do next, Sarge?” one asked.

Sergeant Baros looked them over, thinking while he, at last, took a big sip of coffee. “What we don’t do is go back to the rail yard. Tate will be long gone by now. He may have caught one of the trains pulling out after we left. We have to send out alerts, and we have to interrogate the man we caught. By the way, his name is Tommy Thomson. He just hasn’t admitted it yet.”

Dave Wentworth cleared his throat and partially raised his hand before speaking. “Sargent Baros,” he ventured. “Why not take Jazzy back down there and finish the tracking. We can’t be sure he’s not still around the tracks some place, can we?”

"True enough, Dave," Sergeant Baros said, thinking the same thing before the Captain had pulled them all away.

Dave nodded but then had another thought. "I forgot to say goodby to Hope before she left. Please tell her for me how much I enjoyed her help today."

Sergeant Baros' cup was put down hard, and he glanced at the ceiling trying to think this out. "I didn't take her home, Dave," he blurted. "I thought you did…." he trailed off and reached for the phone and quietly dialed his home number. They all heard the ringing coming from the handset. No one answered. Hope was not home.

Chapter Six

Night Ride

Hope stood in the center of the boxcar, her arms spread widely along with her feet. She swayed from side to side as the train gathered speed. Jazzy was seated in front of her, watching her face attentively. Her fear of the strange man intensified in the near darkness, the only light being filtered through gaps in the door as well as along scattered vent holes near the roof. Noise and clatter from the steel wheels beneath her feet intensified as the train reached its intended speed. Hope looked around, squinting to make out details, finally recognizing a set of steel rungs leading up near one corner of the car. Above the ladder was the outline of a hatch of some sort. As she studied it, thinking of escape, it came to her that the man they had seen could use this hatch to shoot down at them, and there would be no place to hide. She wondered if there was a latch on the inside, but in the near darkness, she couldn't see any details.

She made her way across the moving floor and stood under the hatch, holding on to the ladder. There seemed to be a handle on the inner side of the hatch, but she realized that the ladder would have to be climbed to try the latch. Hope grabbed the steel ladder and held on, thinking it through before ascending. The swaying would be much worse near the top, and she hesitated, not quite finding the courage to go up.

At that moment, there was a progression of loud banging sounds as slack in the couplings was taken up by slowing of the train. High pitched squealing came from underneath as the brakes were applied. The train slowed and then she felt the push to one side as the train slowly came around a bend. Hope realized that this was her moment to act, and she started up the ladder, her shoulder bumping against the rusted wall of the boxcar. Finally at the top, she took hold of the handle and pulled as hard as she could. The latch slowly engaged just as the train started gaining speed again. Finally, she could relax. They couldn't get out, but the strange man couldn't get in either.

Back on the floor, she patted Jazzy's head and spoke to him with a trace of anger in her voice. "Jazzy, see what you got us into? We don't know where we are going, we have no money, and there is a crazy man out there wanting to hurt us. And…it's all your fault!" Immediately, she regretted her anger toward Jazzy. He was just trying to do his duty and catch the fugitive. Then it hit her, and she saw the situation clearly. Jazzy had found and taken down a man, but it wasn't the one he was tracking. Pop and the other policemen have captured the wrong one. The fugitive from prison was probably riding the same train as they were and would know that Jazzy could and would track him down once he got free. Hope let out a big sigh and slowly lowered herself onto a patch of loose straw. Jazzy lay beside her and placed his big head on her lap. Whatever happened, they were together and Jazzy would protect her. She knew that and so did Jazzy.

As the train rumbled its way through the great plains of the Midwest, day gave way to night, and any meager available light in the boxcar transitioned to complete darkness. It was so black inside that Hope couldn't even see her feet, nor Jazzy. But she felt his cold nose touch her frequently, and all she had to do to contact him was to extend her arm. She rested against the cold wall, trying to get comfortable, and occasionally drifted off to sleep, awakening briefly to become aware of the train horn or the swaying car, then falling backward into her flickering dreams. And in those dreams, there was light and warmth, and her father's kind face bending over her, assuring her that he was there for her and would always be so. Then the momentary awakening, realizing that her back was hurting and cold and that the train was getting further and further away from her home. The despair would clutch her, pummel her and hold her in its grasp until she fell asleep again to escape back into her previous world.

As some scant light seeped into the moving boxcar, Jazzy sprang to his feet, his attention on the overhead hatch. Hope awakened enough to see him standing there, his teeth showing and a low threatening growl vibrating from his body. Hope's brain surged to fully awake, realizing that there must be some threat coming from the hatch. And indeed, there was a subtle noise, a metallic sound which rose above the train noise, a sound that indicated someone was trying to open the hatch from above.

Hope rose to her feet and watched the hatch just as Jazzy was doing. After a few moments the sound went away as the train noise rose again to hide any other sounds. Someone was on the roof of the boxcar trying to open the hatch while the train was still underway. It had to be Tate. He was riding the train with them, intent on keeping Jazzy from tracking him whatever way he could.

The day began long and hot inside the boxcar. There was no food or water and no way out. Hope considered the hatch again, longingly looking at it and thinking about how to get back down to the ground if she managed to open it. Then there was Tate…was he up there lurking about? Nope, going through the hatch wasn't going to happen. Hope sank down again, her back against the wall, her head supported by her hands and arms. Where were they, and where were they going?

There was a change from outside the train. It had been slowing gradually for part of an hour, and now there were sounds which could only be made by other trains. They were not stopped yet, but it seemed to Hope that the train was winding down, about to come to a full stop. Occasionally, she could hear voices and the sounds of trucks. It reminded her of the rail yard they had originally come from. Could they have returned, she hoped?

With a jerk, the train fully stopped amid the sound of its couplings compressing. They both intently listened, expecting to hear voices coming their way.

Chapter Seven

Just Another Rail Yard

Hope started to despair. It seemed hours ago that the train had stopped. A couple of times they could hear voices of the railroad workers and train engines huffing into the distance, but their car was left standing right where it stopped. She looked again at the hatch…wondering. Yes, she would chance it, there was no other choice.

Hand over hand, she climbed toward the handle she had secured previously. This time, it disengaged more easily, and afterward she could tell that the hatch would lift away if she pushed it hard enough. Jazzy was directly below her, intently watching her every move.

“Jazzy,” she said softy. “I’m going through, and in a few minutes I’ll open the door and let you out. I promise I won't forget." Jazzy looked back at her without moving, a furry statue attached to the floor. Then Hope pushed hard and sunlight streamed in as well as fresh air. She tentatively put her head out and looked around. They were no longer attached to a locomotive and instead parked on a side track. In the distance she could see activity and smoke from several engines. And gratefully, there was no sign of Tate anywhere around. Just on the other side of the hatch was another ladder, this time headed toward the ground.

After a bit of excitement getting on the steel ladder, she made it nearly to the ground and dropped the rest of the way. In the sunlight, she could see that her pure white sweater was heavily soiled with soot and dirt as were her pants and shoes. She found the sliding door and saw a pin wedged in the lock mechanism. Once removed, the door slid open enough to let Jazzy explode through. He shook himself off and seemed to be smiling at her. For once, she had saved him instead of the other way around. "Jazzy," she said firmly, “stay beside me, and I won’t clip you into the leash. I can trust you, can’t I?” One look at Jazzy’s face said what words could never convey. She could trust Jazzy completely, even with her life, if it came to that.

Together, they started walking down the track, not knowing what they would encounter, but whatever it was, it would be better than another day inside a moving boxcar.

By the time Hope noticed a group of rail yard workers standing together, she realized that they were all watching her and Jazzy. As she closed the distance to them, one man called out to her. “Hey, what are you doing here? Did you just get out of a boxcar?” Hope nodded a yes, but she wasn’t sure he had seen her answer. “Did you hear me?” the man asked with more anger and started moving toward her.

“I’d advise you to stay where you are. My dog wouldn’t like it if you get too close,” she said. She could hear the low growl but doubted if the man could. He did notice the dog though and came to a stop several yards away.

"What are you doing here, Miss?" he asked.

"We were locked in a boxcar behind us and have been traveling for more than a day. I don't even know where we are," Hope replied.

"Can I ask how you got in there in the first place?"

"A man named Tate escaped from prison and locked us in there. Then the train took off."

The worker took off his cap and scratched his head, then turned to the group behind him, "One of you guys go get the supervisor. Miss, if you and your dog will walk with me, I'll lead you over there and let him handle this."

"What is your name?" Hope asked.

“Bob,” he answered. Looking a bit sheepish. “Sorry I was rude, Miss, before I mean. What is your name?”

“I am called Hope, and this is Jazzy.” she said patting his head.

“When we first spotted you, I have to admit it was a shock. Seeing a pretty girl amid all this rolling stock…I thought I was dreaming for a moment. Then I saw the dog. Mighty big and dangerous dog. Sure you can handle him?”

“I don’t really control him. He does what he wants at times but mostly does what I want him to do. He just seems to know,” Hope answered. “He was a police dog and now he is mine.”

“Don’t worry, the way he is looking at me, I wouldn’t dare to get any closer.” They started walking slowly toward a group of buildings, Bob in the lead.

Frequently, Bob would look back and reassure himself that they were staying behind him. There was an older man approaching from the front. He wore a large brimmed hat over a white shirt with suspenders. The man stopped to talk to Bob before acknowledging Hope and Jazzy. Then he started moving toward them. Hope noticed that the man had a pronounced limp and was smiling at them.

"So you found us, and we found you!" he exclaimed. Jazzy was watching the man closely but there were no threats from him this time. "I would guess that you are Hope and her dog, Jazzy." Am I right?" he asked. "In case you are wondering, I heard your name from Bob just now, but I have had calls about you all morning. We had no idea that you were here, but now it all makes a lot of sense."

"Was that my dad who was calling?" Hope asked.

"No one said anything about being your dad. The entire police force in your town is looking under every rock for you. Now I understand. Your dad is a policeman then?"

"Sergeant Baros," Hope answered. "Will you tell him we are here?"

"I sure will, Hope. Right away, too. Say, did you know how far you traveled in that boxcar?"

"No, and I don't even know which direction we went. But I'll bet Jazzy knows."

"I'm certain of that as well. It's a shocker, but you traveled about three hundred miles. A train doesn't go very fast, but the miles just roll by. Say, until your dad gets here you need some place to rest up and eat. Both of you do. I live about two miles from here, and my wife, Jill, is a grand old gal, and we would love to have you rest there until your Dad comes."

"And Jazzy also?" Hope asked.

"Sure thing. We love dogs, especially big ones. Jazzy is welcome. Oh, and I am Superintendent Falls, but you can call me Jack if you will."

"I need to tell you something important, Jack," Hope said, and waited until she got his full attention. "We were tracking a man named Jerome Tate who escaped from prison. Jazzy caught one of them yesterday, but I'm very sure Tate was the man who locked us in the boxcar, and during the night I heard somebody trying to open the hatch from outside. Have you seen any strangers around here other than us?"

Jack took off his hat and banged the dust off of it, squinting into the distance. "We always find some hobos who like to catch a ride for free, and we run them off. I did hear the men found one early this morning and told him to git. Never saw him myself. Guess he could have been the man you were looking for."

Chapter Eight

A Touch of Home

Once out of the car, Hope stood in front of Jack's house and looked around. It was picturesque, just as if it was a painting on a postcard. The lawn and shrubs were trimmed neatly, and there were blooming flowers everywhere. A covered porch wrapped around two sides and behind the house were acres of crops, stretching into the distance. The house was constructed of wood and older but in perfect condition, and through the windows could be seen more plants and flowers behind the glass.

"Wow," Hope said and smiled, turning to Jack who was smiling back. "It's just like a storybook!" When she resumed looking at the house, an aproned woman was coming out of the front door. The woman was smiling broadly and waving at them.

“Well, welcome and hello. You must be Hope and Jazzy,” she said, getting closer. “Looks like you need some attention, young lady. A bath and clean clothes would be nice, I think. Are you hungry as well?” She went around Hope in a circle inspecting her dirty and soiled clothes and tsk, tsking as she went. “We have some clothes that will fit you while I wash your things, Dear. Come inside and we will get you cleaned up.”

Hope raised her hand to get attention before speaking. “What about Jazzy? Can he come with me? And what should I call you?”

“I was named Maybelle and that’s what Jack calls me. Most pronounce it Mable and that’s OK by me. Oh yes, your dog is welcome inside, and we’ll even feed him too. Come on in and let’s start getting clean and fed.”

After seating herself at the dinner table, Hope looked around at the abundance of fresh food before her. After all, she and Pop eat because they had to, not just for dining pleasure. It was a new and welcome experience. Maybelle had fed Jazzy before supper while in the kitchen, and now he was laying just beside her chair, on his side snoring loudly.

“Seems you wore out poor Jazzy,” Jack observed. “He’s sure devoted to you…won’t leave you alone for a second. You said he was a police dog way back when…and retired. So what brought him back into that search you were talking about?”

“They had three dogs searching the other trains but needed Jazzy also. I don’t think Jazzy wanted to be there, but he got one of them right away. I heard you talking to somebody about me before supper. Were you speaking to my Dad?” Hope asked.

“Oh yes, it was your daddy all right, and he was very happy you are safe. He said he will be here before noon tomorrow to pick both of you up," Jack explained.

"That means I'm going to sleep here tonight?" Hope asked.

"We have an extra room since Albert left. You will find it very comfortable, and Jazzy can park himself in there with you," Maybelle said.

"You both have been so kind to us. I don't know how to thank you. Is there anything I can do to earn my keep while I'm here?" Hope asked.

Jack cleared his throat and smiled, "I don't exactly know how to say this to you, Hope, but there is a rather selfish reason we opened our home to you." He glanced at Maybelle before further explanation and watched as her eyes opened wider, obviously not knowing what her husband was about to say.

“Our nearest town is about ten miles from here, and it’s not a big city but always seems to us as brimming with people. To tell the truth, Hope, you are the prettiest…no, I really meant the most beautiful, young woman that I think I ever saw. You make us feel young again just being around you. You see that we both like flowers, I guess. Well, it’s the same feeling around a girl like you. I hope that I didn’t embarrass you, and I’m sure you have heard this before many times. But I just had to tell you what I was thinking, and I’m sure Maybelle feels the same way.”

Hope could feel her face flush, and for a moment her mind raced around with the profound compliments she was hearing. No, she had not previously heard those words used regarding her appearance. Her father was not given to those kinds of compliments. He may have felt that way but would never have told her. The only thing he ever said as a compliment was that she reminded him of her mother. She had seen the few photographs of her mother that had been saved, and indeed, her mother had been very attractive.

"Thank you for saying that, and I do believe you are sincere, but no, I have never heard that before. Frankly, I was raised as a tomboy and never had the slightest pretension to be anything but that," Hope said and then started tearing.

"I feel the same way about you that Jack does, Dear. He is right, of course, about your looks, but there is more about you than just looks. You are delicate yet strong, smart yet shy. Pretty soon you will need old Jazzy over there to protect you from boys. I just want you to be ready when it comes. But since we are on that subject, I can't help from being angry that your daddy allowed you to go in harm's way, dog or no dog. Thinking about it, I get mad," Maybelle said with some force, and she leaned forward in a display of protectiveness that caught Hope by surprise.

"It wasn't Pop's fault. He didn't want me involved, even ordered me to the car. It was Jazzy's rules we had to play by. He knew he had to do his job, but he could not part with me for even a second, especially if there were bad people around. He loves me more than anything. Now, let me at least help do the dishes," Hope said and pushed back from the table.

Chapter Nine

YOU CAN RUN BUT

There was a gentle morning breeze coming in the partially open window, along with ample sunlight. In the distance were nearly continuous sounds of earth being worked by large tractors. Hope opened her eyes slightly, still not aware of her present location, but the bed was warm and soft, and the colors in the room enchanting in the speckled light of morning. Some weight was being applied to the side of the bed, and she laughed before reaching out to pet his big head. "Jazzy, you wonderful big loyal dog of mine…." She looked toward that side and saw a familiar sight. He had placed his head far enough on the bed that his nose was lying against her arm. The love in his eyes impacted her more forcefully than usual. She noticed the gray whiskers on his chin, a sign that Jazzy was heading toward his later years and would probably not be there when she finally reached adulthood. What a gift it was to have him around when she needed him the most. "Ready for breakfast, Jazzy?" she asked and received a small bark in return. She was sure he understood her words, not just their meaning.

After breakfast, she again helped with the dishes and talked almost continuously with Maybelle who quickly was becoming something between a friend and a mother. In her heart, Hope wished that these two wonderful people could be relatives of hers whom she could visit with from time to time.

"Hope," Maybelle began, "Your father isn't due to arrive for at least two hours." She paused, thinking out her request. Hope was looking at her, waiting on the second part. "Would you walk with me up the road a bit this morning? I have to pick up some produce from a neighbor, and I'm sure you will like meeting that family." Hope nodded a yes but felt that there was more to the story and didn't look away. "And, they have a son about your age…" Maybelle finally disclosed what the trip was really about. "Oh," she continued after a thoughtful pause, "and he is rather good-looking himself." Maybelle looked a bit shy after telling the whole story, and she looked out the window while expecting some reply from Hope.

"I never mind meeting good-looking boys. We can go anytime you say," Hope replied.

It was only about half a mile between houses. But these neighbors were full-time farmers, not a railroad family, and their farm was very alive with activity. As the three got closer, the sound of farm machinery grew ever louder. There was a bit of dust in the air created by a big tractor tilling up soil in the distance. Hope became aware that there was something happening to Jazzy, and she started watching him instead of concentrating on the views. Jazzy had moved somewhat ahead of them. His head was up, and he was sniffing the air. His head moved back and forth as if he had become interested in what was around and ahead of him. Hope reached down and stroked his back, but he ignored her, never looking back as he usually did. Something was up, and it was obvious that Jazzy was detecting some interesting scents. Hope started to grow agitated considering what it could mean.

"Maybelle, can you tell me who works at this farm we are heading toward?" Hope asked.

"Well, it's a family farm so the entire family works there. But in active periods of farming they will occasionally hire an additional man or two. Is that what you wanted to know?"

"It's what I expected to hear. Maybelle, I've got to tell you something before we get there," Hope said with a near whisper. Maybelle stopped walking and turned to face her, starting to dread hearing whatever Hope was going to say. "Back home, Jazzy and the policemen were trying to catch an escaped convict named Jerome Tate. He got away, and I'm pretty sure that he was the one that locked us in the boxcar, and I think he tried to open the overhead hatch that night.

Watching Jazzy, I'm starting to think that Tate came this way recently."

Maybelle's hand came up to her mouth, and her eyes widened in surprise. "Why in the world would this man want to do you harm, Hope?" she asked.

"Because Jazzy knows his scent and can track him down, that's why. He's afraid of this dog."

"We should go back and call Jack. He will know what to do," Maybelle said.

"It's too late for that. Look at Jazzy. He is already tracking Tate's scent. I don't think he will turn around now. We have to go where he goes because I don't want to go back without him and neither do you," Hope explained and could see that Maybelle was nodding in agreement. They would be unprotected back home without Jazzy.

As the three continued to walk toward the farm, they began to see individuals moving about doing their various jobs. It was still too far away to make out faces, but Hope was concentrating, trying to be alert and recognize Tate before they were spotted by him. Jazzy stopped moving forward and gave Hope a prolonged stare. He was trying to tell her something. What he wanted suddenly became obvious, he wanted the leash unclipped. Hope briefly wondered if there was some telepathy at play: could Jazzy actually be that intelligent?

Hope bent down and unclipped him. Jazzy continued to focus on the farm, watching the men moving around and frequently sniffing the air. Abruptly, Jazzy moved off the road to be alongside a tall growth of corn, completely out of view of the farm and anyone watching. He continued forward, often looking back toward Hope as a signal to follow him. It dawned on Hope what Jazzy's plan was all about. In her fresh white sweater, accompanied by a big dog, they would instantly be spotted by Tate, giving him the advantage. This way, they would get much closer before Tate became alarmed.

"Is that dog doing what I think he is doing?" Maybelle wondered, taking it all in.

"Amazing, isn't he?" Hope agreed.

"There is only one word for that dog," Maybelle said with certainty. "Predator."

Tate was there all right, and he was watching the two women advance toward the farm. He noticed the girl in the white sweater and looked at her for a moment or two, wondering if she was familiar or not. The key ingredient was the big dark dog. This girl had no dog, and the dog was the one who would be dangerous, the one who could positively identify him. He reflexly patted his pocket containing the gun, assuring himself that it was still there. Then he went back to his work.

The entrance to the farm was just ahead and about even with the rows of nearly mature corn stalks. Hope glanced toward Jazzy just in time to see him disappearing into a row only two deep from the front edge of the tall stalks. She cast her eyes about, looking at each man in view. One stood out and the more she looked, the more her memory brought back the moment he was framed in the door of the boxcar. He was Tate for sure, and he was the reason Jazzy had become invisible.

Tate stopped working to get a better look at the two women headed toward the farm. One was older, and he was sure he had never before encountered her. But the other one…the younger blonde wearing a white sweater…raised his eyebrows. She was starting to trigger a memory though he only got a glance at her in a dark corner before he shut the door. It could be…

What Tate was not watching was the row of corn stalks only a hundred feet away. In-between the stalks was the dark head of a big dog waiting on the perfect moment to close the distance as quickly as possible, his muscles tensed, his body crouched low and his eyes focused on his target.

It takes a fast, trained and conditioned human about ten seconds to cover one hundred meters traveling at around fourteen miles an hour. A muscular dog will take under half that time. Even if you are already looking his way, it would take some time to react to a charge, but seeing him come at you out of your peripheral vision… And so, Tate saw him coming only for two seconds before he arrived. There was no barking or growling giving warning. Not enough time to do anything but scream…while he could.

Hope and Maybelle arrived at the moment Tate started screaming. The others present at first looked up in surprise, then started running in different directions and for different reasons. Hope could see Tate's feet and Jazzy standing over him waiting on his next movement. She called “Come, Jazzy,” and when that had no effect she ordered “Jazzy, *Fuss*.” Also with no effect. There was a pistol lying on the ground near Tate’s feet, but Hope didn’t want to get that close. Behind her she could hear Maybelle loudly trying to explain what just happened.

“Yes,” Maybelle said. “Call the police but leave the dog alone. He may have just saved your lives!”

Hope couldn’t hear the answer but the angry voices she understood, and she realized that these folks had no idea of whom they had hired or why Jazzy had attacked the man so suddenly.

Sergeant Baros happened to arrive just before the police cruiser from the opposite direction started pulling in. There were two groups of people present: three men were standing together watching Jazzy, and the other group was talking to Hope and an older woman. Baros pulled on his police hat and pinned his badge to his shirt before getting out of the car. He made his way toward Hope first and as soon as she saw him, she was in his arms, tears wetting her face.

"What happened, Hope?" Pop asked, smoothing her hair away from her face.

"Jazzy got him, Pop. He's lying down over there, and Jazzy won't come away. Everybody here is afraid that Jazzy will attack them also."

"No, he won't attack anybody. Come with me, and we'll get him away from harm." They walked toward Jazzy who was watching them intently but still glancing back to the man on the ground.

Sergeant Baros got close enough to see that Tate's eyes were open but also saw the wounds on both arms. "Tate, you are under arrest. Do not move, understand?

He turned to Jazzy and petted his head. "Good job, my friend, good job. You can go to Hope now, you are done here." Jazzy didn't hesitate, without a backward look he trotted over to Hope and placed his head affectionally against her leg, looking up to her with adoration in his eyes.

The End